My Adoption Story, A Baby's Journey
ESP That's Me!

Written by Annie-Bug

This book is dedicated to my grandson, E.S.P. who was adopted into our family. He sent out that message for his parents to find him.

It was Bashert…or meant to be.

I am in a dark, warm place where I know I am safe.

It was meant to be.

Where do you feel safe?

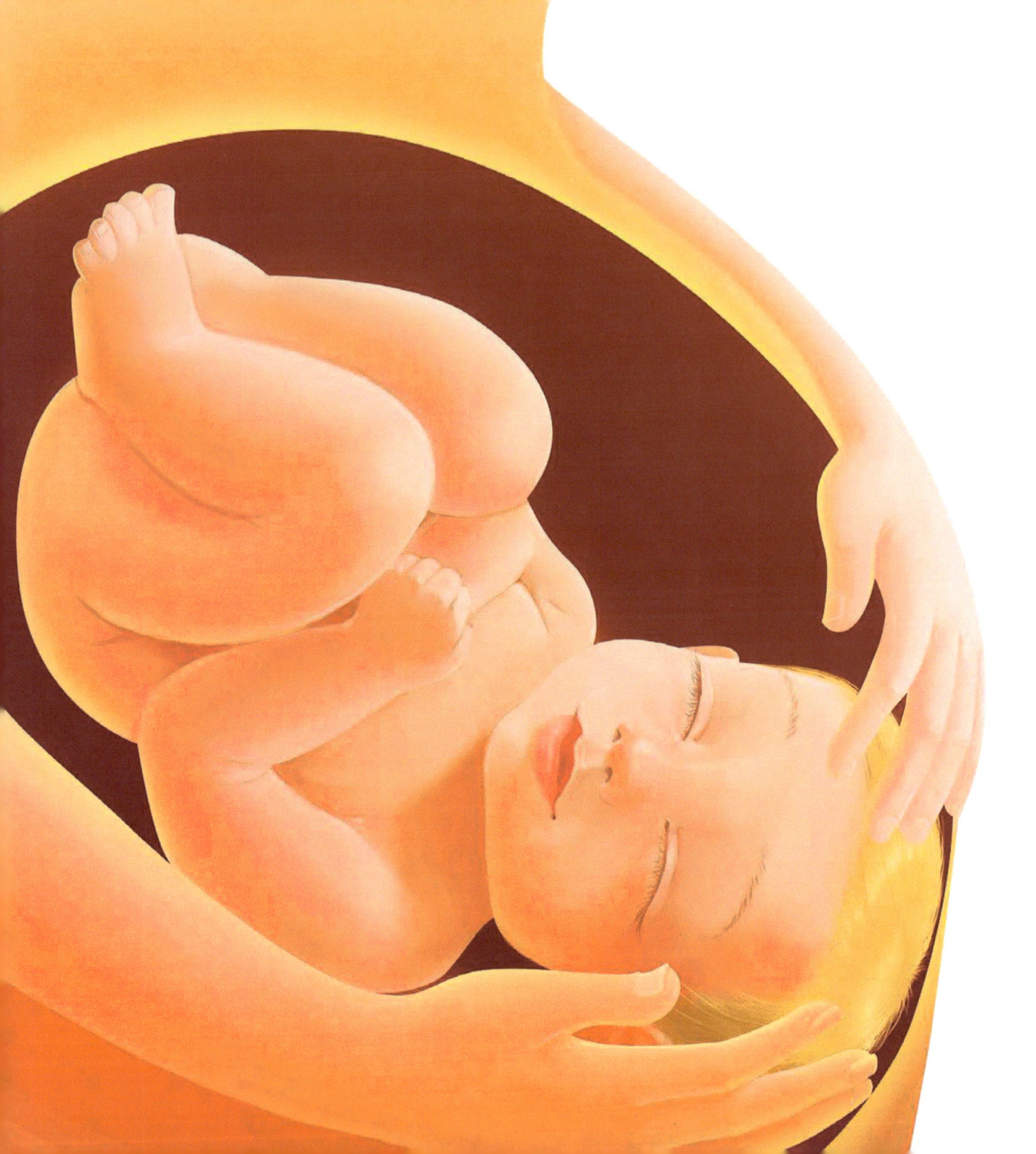

I am growing in my birth Mommy's tummy.

I know I won't live here forever, all by myself.

It was meant to be.

Are you ever by yourself?

All day and night I hear my birth Mommy's heartbeat go "swoosh, swoosh."

It makes me sleepy, so I take a nap.

It was meant to be.

When do you take a nap?

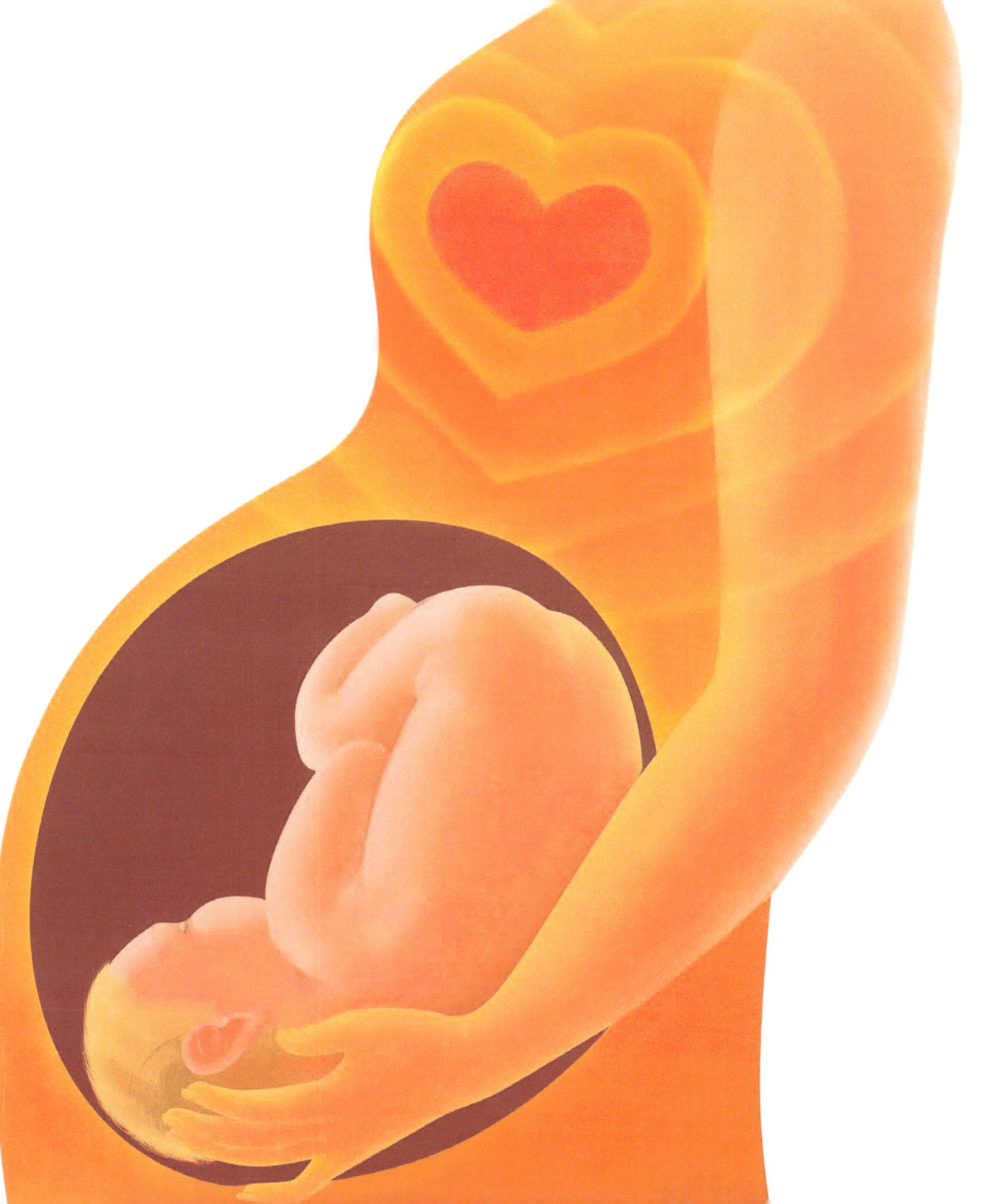

Sometimes I wake up and I hear
my birth Mommy crying.

I know she is sad because she cannot
keep me to live with her always.

It was meant to be.

When do you cry?

I know that my birth Mommy loves me, but I cannot stay with her forever.

It was meant to be.

Who loves you?

I know that my forever Mommy and Daddy will be coming to meet me very soon.
That is when I will get adopted.

It was meant to be.

Can you guess what adopted means?

I know that being adopted is very special.

Adopted means that my birth Mommy and Daddy choose a different Mommy and Daddy to be my forever Mommy and Daddy.

It was meant to be.

Are you adopted?

I sent a message to them—a kind of wish by thinking very hard. Some people call it E.S.P.

That way they can find me here at the hospital.

It was meant to be.

Do you ever wish for something?

I am getting very excited to meet my parents.

I know they will be exactly the right people to love me and I will love them right back!

It was meant to be.

When do you get excited?

Today is the day that I am born!

I know it will be cold at first, but they will
wrap me in a blanket and put
a blue cap on my head to make me warm.

What do you think the blue cap means?

Am I a boy or girl?

Slowly, I open my eyes and I see two people looking at me.

They have tears in their eyes and smiles on their faces.

It was meant to be.

Are they happy or sad?

I know who they are!
They got my message.

It was meant to be.

Do you know who they are?

"Hi, little man," he says to me.
"Do you know who we are?"

I know who they are, but they tell me anyway.

It was meant to be.

Who do you think they are?

"We are your Mommy and Daddy.
We have only just met you and already
we love you very, very much."

It was meant to be.

Who do you love?

Then my Mommy holds me in her arms and I can hear her heartbeat go "swoosh, swoosh."

She tells me, "You make our family complete."

It was meant to be.

Who is in your family?

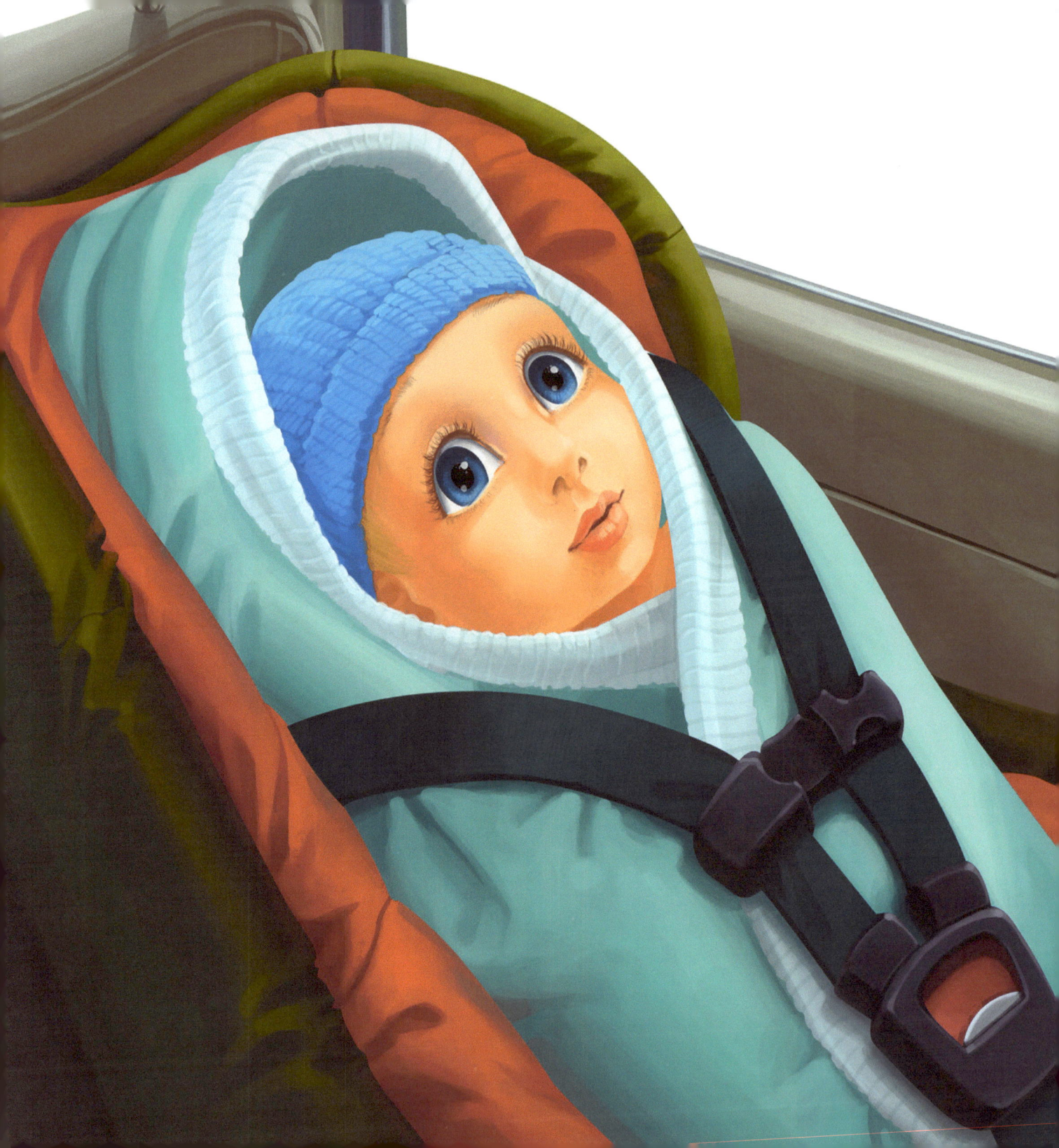

Today I get to meet the world!
My Mommy and Daddy put me in my car seat and drive me home.
I know this is where I am going to grow up and I can't wait!

It was meant to be.

Where do you live?

Now I am part of a family—the Parkers.
I am so happy.

My name is Eric Skyler Parker and my initials are E.S.P.
That is how I sent my wish!

Look at all the people waiting for me!
I have grandparents, aunts, uncles and cousins too.

It was meant to be.

How happy do you think I am?

What makes you happy?

www.ingramcontent.com/pod-product-compliance
Lightning Source LLC
Chambersburg PA
CBHW040021130526
44590CB00036B/50